Pilot Jane

and the Runaway Plane

BIG SUNSHINE BOOKS

Bright Books for Bright Minds

Once there was a daring pilot called Jane,

Who travelled the world in her cool pink plane.

Over cities, mountains and seas she'd roam,

Carrying her passengers safely home.

Pilot Jane's best friend was her plane called Rose,

An aircraft with flowers, tailfin to nose.

Rose loved to race and her engine was fast.

"Go girls!" she'd whoop as she thundered on past!

Fastest Plane

Each day the friends saw exciting places,
Action, adventure – many new faces!

And wherever Jane went, Rose was there too,

Singing this song as they shot through the blue:

WHOOSH! Let's fly up, up and away!

Jane and Rose are your team today.

We're smart! We're strong! An awesome pair,

Come rain or shine, we'll get you there!

Whatever the weather, we work together

In good times and bad . . . *Girl Power Forever!*

On **Monday**, Jane and Rose are off to **Rome.**

Then to **Paris,** before travelling home.

On **Tuesday** in **Beijing** there's lots to see.
Jane practises Chinese . . . and then tai chi.

On Wednesday,
the friends fly on to Brazil.

On Thursday...
Alaska! *Brrrrrr* – what a chill!

There's snow in New York
and fog in Hong Kong...

But still those brave girls go zipping along!

Phew! Then in **Sydney** there's time for a break.

Surfer Jane rides the waves . . .

Rose sends for **cake**.

CAKE FUEL

Now the excited girls must get some rest,

For tomorrow they have a special guest!

The **Queen** must fly to a party in haste.

She's asked for the girls – there's no time to waste!

But during the night, poor Rose feels unwell
With a horrible bug nothing can quell.
"Uh-oh!" she cries. "My engine's spluttering!
My wings are sore; my tummy's fluttering."

"I'm sorry, Jane, it's plane flu I fear . . .
Cake fuel was **not** the best idea!
I'm overheating and feeling yucky.
How could this happen? It's SO unlucky!"

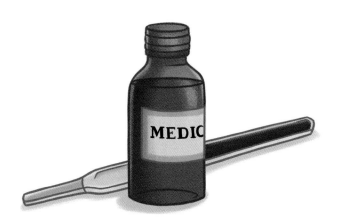

The next day Rose had to stay in her bed.
"I've let the Queen down!" the sorry plane said.

"Engine failure!" the engineer cried.

"Jane, it's a shame Rose can't be at your side."

"Now we'll need to find you another jet.

We can get the Queen to this party yet!

Let me show you the speedy Mighty Mitch.

He'll carry the Queen there without a hitch."

Mitch was the biggest plane she'd ever seen,
A GIGANTIC, lean, mean flying machine.
Mitch groaned: "A girl pilot! Bother and drat!
I'll bet she's slow – or a big scaredy-cat!"

"What a cheek!" thought Jane, who was not amused.
"Mighty Mitch must be mightily confused."
Aloud she said only, "Come fly with me!
We girls can surprise you, I guarantee!"

Later, Mighty Mitch sped down the runway.

Dark clouds were looming – no time to delay!

*Z*OOM! He took off with a deafening roar.

And as they climbed, the Queen started to snore!

But once in the air, Mitch raced through the cloud.
He **looped** and **swooped**,
feeling clever and proud.

Naughty Mitch thought he'd show Jane who was boss . . .
But his troublesome tricks made her so cross!

Rain started falling –
Mitch flew left . . . then right.
Jane gripped the controls
to steady the flight.

Mitch played with his flaps;
Jane started to frown.
The Queen, bumped awake,
held tight to her crown!

Then came a CRASH! and flash of bright lightning.

Mighty Mitch yelped, "This storm's getting frightening!"

He changed direction without warning Jane . . .

Mighty Mitch was now

a runaway plane!

"STOP, MITCH!"

Jane cried. "Though this storm is no breeze,

My **skill** and your **speed** can beat it with ease.

Rather than fighting, let's work **together**

To make it through this terrible weather!"

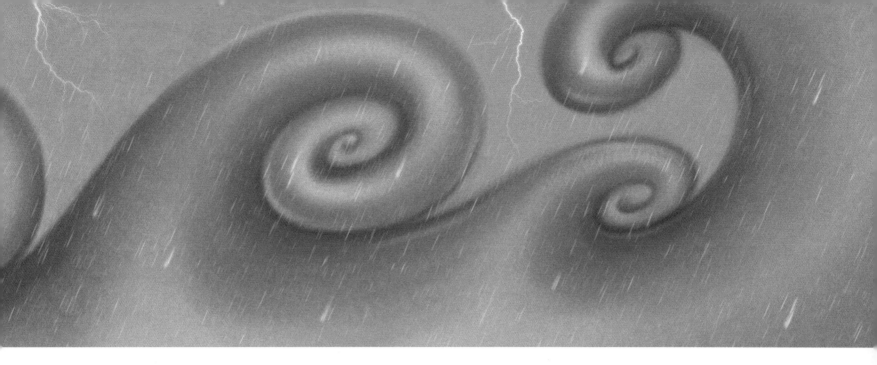

And so they started to work as a **team**,

Jane steering, Mitch weaving – then, like a dream . . .

They shot through the cloud, Mitch at full throttle.

"**Amazing!**" he cried. "This **girl's** got bottle!"

Minutes later, they had safely touched down.

The Queen smoothed her hair and righted her crown.

"Yikes!" she cried. "That was a pretty close call.

PHEW! I'll get to my party after all!"

"Let's give a big cheer for Pilot Jane
And Mitch, her mighty, magnificent plane.
Hip hip hooray! Hip hip hooray!
Brave Jane and Mitch have saved the day!"

Now Mitch is a **kinder**, more **helpful** plane,
Who greatly admires his new friend Jane.

And, happily, Rose feels better now too,
You might even see her flying near you!

Best of all, when the girls next had a break
The **Queen** invited them for tea . . . and **cake!**

So if you're out, take a look at the sky,
Friends **Jane** and **Rose** could be travelling by!
Together again and racing along,
Exploring the world and singing this song:

WHOOSH! Let's fly up, up and away!

Jane and Rose are your team today.

We're smart! We're strong! An awesome pair,

Come rain or shine, we'll get you there!

Whatever the weather, we work together,

Hooray for *Girl* - and *Boy* - *Power forever!*

To Joseph and Annie, with love – CB

To my father, with love – IC

BIG SUNSHINE BOOKS

First published in the UK in 2017 by Big Sunshine Books Ltd
61 Godstow Road, Wolvercote, Oxford OX2 8PE
www.bigsunshinebooks.com

Text copyright © 2017 Caroline Baxter
Illustrations copyright © 2017 Izabela Ciesinska
Edited by Blue Elephant Storyshaping

ISBN: 978-1-910854-03-7

A CIP catalogue record for this book is available from the British Library.

1 3 5 7 9 10 8 6 4 2

Printed in China